Anansi's Narrow Waist

**An African folk tale
retold by Len Cabral
Illustrated by David Diaz**

GoodYear Books

One day Anansi the spider
smelled yams cooking.
"Mmm, I love yams!" he said.

Anansi didn't want to wait.
"Tie a string around my waist,"
he said.

"Tug the string when the yams are done. Then I'll come back."

5

Anansi kept walking.

He smelled rice and beans cooking.

"Mmm, I love rice and beans!" he said.

"Come," the people shouted.
"We'll eat soon."

Anansi didn't want to wait.
"Tie a string around my waist,"
he said.

"Tug the string when the rice and beans are done. Then I'll come back."

9

Anansi kept moving deeper into the jungle.

Soon he had eight strings tied
to his waist.

He felt a tug. "Oooh! Yams!" he said.
Another tug. "Oooh! Rice and beans!"
he said.

He felt another tug and then another.

The strings got
tighter and tighter.

Then they **snapped!**

Now you know why spiders have eight legs and very narrow waists.